LALITA AND OTHER
SHORT STORIES

The Unseen Women Of India

Aarti Punjabi

DEDICATION

For My Mother

A strong woman who never lets adversities get the better of her

Lalita And Other Short Stories

CONTENTS

Lalita And Other Short Stories

ACKNOWLEDGMENTS

I would not have managed to do this without the love, support, and blessings of my family and friends. I am grateful to Blogchatter; it was on this platform that I started sharing my stories and received tremendous support from the community during the pandemic. My husband, Manoj, and children, Chirag and Tanya, for cheering me at every step. My friends who (you know who you are) believed in me more than I did.

A big thank you to my sister Deepika for encouraging me to take this leap, Devika for helping me with the cover, Sreeni for reading the drafts, and Chandana and Preetika for patiently listening to my rant.

Thank you, dear reader, for taking the time to read this anthology. I hope you enjoy these stories that were waiting to be told.

Somewhere or other there must surely be
The face not seen; the voice not heard...

Christina Rosetti

The life of a flower is longing and fulfilment.

A tear and a smile.

Khalil Gibran

LALITA

Lalita could not stop smiling as she adjusted the pleats on her saree; she liked them crisp and neat. She looked at herself in the small square mirror on the wall and combed her hair. Just three more days and then she would leave for Mankapur. Her niece, Muniya, was getting married and the groom lived in a city. He was the head peon of LC Girls College in Lucknow and stayed in the staff quarters on the school campus. She could picture Ganga Prasad, Muniya`s groom, touching her feet and seeking her blessings. She beamed with pleasure at the thought and mulled over what she would give as a gift to him. She had some money stashed in between her sarees. Maybe she would give him 200 rupees. After all, she was the bride`s Aunt;

she had to give him something besides the *neg* (cash gift) she would gift him for the wedding. Let me speak to *Amma* and then decide, she thought to herself.

The very thought of *Amma* was comforting. Every year, when she visited *Amma* in Mankapur, days would fly. She felt like a bird who had found her little piece of the sky- no rules, rituals, or objections. No one treated her like an outcast there- she always felt loved and welcomed. She slept till the sun was up, ate, talked, sang, laughed- she lived! Life in her matrimonial home in Lalitpur was rigid, hard, and unbending- just like *Maaji,* her mother-in-law. She would frown- no, make it- scowl- if Lalita even smiled at anyone. For *Maaji,* all Lalita was fit for was menial chores: cleaning the house, washing clothes by the stream, and toiling in the fields. Going to the village fair? No. Talking in an audible voice? Not allowed. Smiling? Forbidden. How could she do all this? She had swallowed her husband barely one year into her marriage. At least, that's what *Maaji* believed, and she reminded her about it now and then.

Baba, her father-in-law, was firm yet gentle. He never raised his voice at her, nor ordered her around like *Maaji.* Lalita often wondered if he even knew what she looked like, as she always pulled her saree over her face when she spotted him. No good daughter-in-law from a respectable family would sit without her pallu drawn over the face in the presence of her in-laws. She moved about the house quietly and efficiently, finishing her chores. As a widow, she had learned to live in the shadows, unseen and unheard.

It was barely six months into her marriage that her husband, Balramdas Shukla, who was in the Army and was posted in Siachen, went missing after a massive avalanche hit his post. After nearly 7 years of being declared missing in action, everyone in the village assumed that he was dead. The village *pandit* suggested a pooja and a *havan* as a final ritual for the departed soul. A host of instructions were mandated for Lalita: dress only in white cotton, no jewelry, *kajal, bindi, or mehendi* allowed, and a mourning period of one year. Her brother and mother came after the one-year mourning period, and *Amma* timidly suggested that Lalita be sent back to Mankapur with her. Baba had firmly declared, "She's our bahu. She will stay with us." That was nearly three years ago. Since then, her life revolved around house chores and farming.

Last year, she had gone to Mankapur to attend her older niece Gudiya's wedding; *Amma* had specially called for sarees from Kanpur and kept a pale blue one for Lalita. She wouldn't dare to drape a colored saree in Lalitpur, but at *Amma's* place, she took the liberty of wearing pale colors and occasionally donning a gold bangle. She had drooled over the tiny white flowers on the soft silky fabric and gently traced the petals and buds. She oiled and tied her hair in a bun but refused to wear the flowers. There was only so much she could dare to do as a young widow. But *Amma* did not see anything wrong in wearing flowers. "He's gone, *beti*, but you are here…" She hugged her mother tight and said, "I am wearing the saree *na*, besides, I don't like wearing flowers in my hair."

***

Lalita had just finished cooking. She hurried through her chores to resume work on the saree she planned to gift her niece: a pale pink organdie saree with delicate rose buds in deep red, bright green stalks and leaves. Muniya had loved the embroidered handkerchief set she had painstakingly embroidered and gifted to Gudiya as a wedding present last summer. Muniya had insisted that at least one handkerchief from the set should be given to her! Lalita had promised to embroider a set for her and was sure this saree would be a much-loved gift for Muniya. Lalita hummed under her breath. *Maaji* was sitting out in the courtyard, deeply engrossed in watching her favourite serial on her phone. Lalita had to be very soft lest she be heard- if she caught a slight humming, also *Maa ji`* would pounce on her, and a volley of harsh comments would pierce her soul. "Look at this *besharmi*! Husband is gone, and this *maharani* is singing."

The TV was blaring in the adjoining room- Baba`s favourite pastime was to listen to news from all over the world. He was leaning against the door leading to the courtyard, snoozing. A gentle breeze provided some respite from the oppressive heat. She could hear that reporter on TV shrieking away. Why was he always so excited, breathless, and screechy? Always screaming-jabbering non-stop like a fast line locomotive.

"Kya aap maan sakte hain??" He sounded almost delirious.

"Haan, maan sakte hai," she muttered, smirking as she tied a knot on the thread. She kept the saree aside and walked up to the almirah to pick out a new bunch of red thread.

Suddenly, she heard Baba shouting, "Rajjo, Rajjo." *Maaji* ran from the courtyard, and Lalita threw the threads and raced towards him. "Ballu, Ballu," Baba was whispering incoherently. Lalita held on to his feet and tried to calm him while *Maaji* cradled his head. He pointed to the screen. Lalita froze as she saw the images on the TV. The motor-mouth reporter raced- "Lance Nayak Balramdas Shukla, who had gone missing in action 10 years back. Perfectly preserved body found in Siachen." She stared blankly at the screen. "Not a scratch on his body...they will contact family." The snippets barely registered in her numb mind.

This cannot happen! Are they out of their minds? 10 years, and they have found his body? Buried under ice? Nonsense. Lalita`s mind whirred with thoughts; how could his body be found after so many years? Who found it? How come his body had not decayed? Maybe he was alive? She shook her head vigorously; wringing her hands, she walked back into her room and shut the door.

***

"Lalita *Ari O* Lalita" - she could hear someone calling her out, banging on the door. She winced as the door hinges rattled and creaked under the pressure. The door swayed and swung in and out, sighing in pain. Lalita had lost track of time- she couldn't recollect how long she had been lying on the floor, curled like a tight ball, staring vacantly at the peeled plaster on the wall. She had tried tracing the cracks going up the wall, or were they coming down? She could not tell. The exercise was futile. She heard snatches of voices. Now and then, a shrill scream or a loud sob fell on her ears, but it did not register or rock her out of her comatose state. Amma wailed incessantly. Snippets of fierce whispers- she couldn't decipher them- then booming voices- as if streaming out from the loudspeaker placed in the village square during festivals- swam around her. Compensation, Poor Woman, Martyr, Injustice, Remarriage, Widow, Evil woman- stray words managed to seep through the dense fog that shrouded her.

Suddenly, the door gave in, and a patch of light illuminated the spot where Lalita lay listless. She felt a shove. Her sister–in–law, Shaano commanded, "Get up! It's time for cremation. You can't keep lying here. Tend to *Maaji.* She is inconsolable." Lalita felt a painful elbow piercing her waist. Adjusting her pallu, she dragged herself, sat on the floor, and started picking at her toenail. Shaano rebuked, "Stop this drama. Have you gone mad? Cover your head. The whole village is here. It is your husband's funeral. Show some grief." Lalita walked out listlessly as the whispers, "No tears, no bawling. What kind of woman she is?" washed over her like the foamy waters of the sea- leaving behind a tingling and stinging sensation.

She shuffled towards the *aangan.* It was packed with people, all trying to catch a glimpse of

Balramdas' face as his dead body lay on the floor covered with flowers. The bright marigold flowers were strewn all over his body. Is this the man I had been married to? She thought to herself as she sat beside him. He looked so different from the grainy pictures she had of him in an album. She touched him the body was cold and stiff. 10 years buried under the snowy, rugged mountains of Siachen, yet so fresh. She gently traced her finger down his arms, and they felt like hard, icy blocks as she moved to the thick blue nerve protruding on his forearm. There was a slight cut on his right cheek -she bent gently to soothe it- suddenly she felt a sharp tug. Shanno whispered angrily "*Besharam* at least cry-shed a few tears-cover your face and STOP touching him." Lalita dutifully followed all the instructions and immediately pulled her hands back; however, the tears took some time to come- a weak trickle dampened her cheeks, soon a torrent followed, and then heavy sobs wracked her thin body. Years of suppression had found a vent in tears, and it rolled out in full force as she clung to his arms. Someone pulled her away, "*Shhh bas bas.*"

There was mayhem all around. She lifted her tear-stained face and looked for comfort. She spotted her brother Chotu standing timidly in one corner. She wanted to run over to him, hug him, and tell him to take her to Mankapur. Then a thought struck her- she would have to miss Muniya's wedding! The wailing became louder. The women around her jostled and whispered, "Poor girl is so shocked. How terrible to become a widow again." Lalita wanted to scream, "I am a widow, but I don't want to miss the wedding." But she knew there was no escaping from these stifling rituals and norms. Surely, she wouldn't be allowed to attend the wedding now. She sobbed and sobbed for all that she had lost once again.

***

Lalita jolted to the present as she heard the *pandit* chant some mantras. She knew it was almost time for cremation. Her body went limp, her shoulders drooped, and her eyes dried up. There are only so many tears you can shed at a time. She was tired. Thoughts kept swirling- maybe she would be homebound for a year again- but then she had already mourned and stayed home for a year last time. Would she have to mourn all over again? She shook with sorrow; her heart raced, and she tried hard to calm herself. Maybe only forty days this time. But what if they insisted on a one-year mourning period?

A fresh wave of panic churned her insides. She would miss Muniya's wedding, and what if they do not allow her to attend her nephew Sohan's wedding, which is eight months away? Where would she wear the saree *Amma* had told her about? A pale pink one this time that Chotu had bought for her from Kanpur that she was supposed to wear for Muniya`s wedding. Lalita had a faraway look in her eyes as she thought about her future. She sat up straight...Why wait for an occasion? Maybe she could wear the saree when she visited Mankapur next. Or she could ask *Amma* to send it over. Then she could wear it whenever she felt like it. She wouldn't let fear of ridicule cripple her anymore. She had performed all her duties. It was time to move on. The worst was already over.

A few men stepped ahead and picked the bier with Balramdas` corpse out of the door *"Ram Naam Satya Hai."* She sighed with relief.

The caged bird sings with a fearful trill
of things unknown but longed for still
and his tune is heard on the distant hill
for the caged bird sings of freedom

Maya Angelou

Jahnvi

A *rrey meri chidiya kahan udi?"* (oh, my little bird, where are you flying off to?) jeered Vijay. Jahnvi tightened her dupatta around her waist and walked out of the kitchen briskly. She banged the main door shut and ran down the six floors. Her heart thumped loudly in her chest. How she hated that creep Vijay and his nasal voice! It was nearly noon, and she would have to rush else, she would be late for school.

She reached home and quickly washed her face. *"Aai,"* (mother) she called out. "Hmm." Her mother's feeble voice grunted. *"Aai,* I won't go to Narang Madam's house from tomorrow. You tell Sulbha *maushi* (Aunt) to go."

"Jaanu, stop troubling your sick mother. It's just a

matter of a few days," her mother rasped.

"I won't go," said Jahnvi firmly as she deftly changed into her school uniform.

"If we tell Sulbha then she gets all the money. Narang Madam will not pay the two of us- only the one who does the work gets paid. If you go instead of me, the money will come to us. You know we need every *paisa* we can manage to earn *beta*." Her mother implored as another bout of cough shook her frail body

"*Aai* that creepy Vijay is horrible," Jahnvi teared up.

"I know he's a *kutta* (dog), but he only barks. He won't bite. I know him. Just make sure you are not alone with him. If he tries anything, scream. That should shut him up," her mother went on, "and *Badi Mummy* (older Aunt) is always home in the mornings. So don't worry. It is just a matter of 3-4 days *beta*. I should recover by then."

Jahnvi sighed in frustration. Her mother always had answers. *Baba* was right. She had an answer for everything! Jahnvi walked out without saying anything. She was running late for her afternoon school. At least her mother allowed her to go to school after she finished her share of household chores. Unlike other girls in her neighborhood, who had dropped out in grade 5 or 6 only as it was difficult to manage studies and household chores,

Jahnvi's mother pushed her to study hard and reminded her now and then, "This is the only way to get out of this drudgery. I don't want you to spend your life tending to others, cleaning, washing, and scrubbing their homes." Her mother had been working as a part-time helper at Narang Madam's house for the last ten years and her meagre earnings ensured they had two square meals most days. Her drunkard father spent his days drinking and occasionally beating up her mother for money to buy more liquor. Jahnvi had to step in for her mother and take over her work at Narang Madam's house, whenever she fell ill – which, of late had been frequent. I am going to study hard, go to college, get a good job in an office, and get out of this mess, she reassured herself.

***

Aai had been sick for nearly a week now. The Narangs lived in a swanky apartment just ahead of their shanties. Now that her mother was sick, Jahnvi had to manage the dusting and mopping of the house. She really didn't mind the job; she actually enjoyed cleaning the house. She picked up the photo frame, wiped the glass gently, and admired the picture of the young girl in it. Hmm in this picture *Didi* looks good- she could be prettier-she does have a bulbous nose- but it's ok, she's sweet to talk to. And she never shouts. Last week, Jahnvi had dropped one of the nail paint bottles, and the paint splattered all over the drawer.

"This was an old one and I didn't like the color much anyway. But be careful from now on, don't go about breaking my things," she had reprimanded her gently Jahnvi picked up the perfume bottles, nail paints, and lipsticks, and lovingly wiped each one clean. She loved the nail paint bottles. Such unusual colours of paint- black, purple, green, yellow-there was even a mud brown! Jahnvi had tried the brown one on her little finger. It looked ugly on her dark skin. Yuck! It was as if she had dipped her finger in wet sticky mud. She wanted to try the black one too but what if *Badi Bhabhi* (elder sister-in-law) noticed? *Badi Bhabhi* was a vulture, with beady eyes, a dark complexion, and a pock-marked face. A surly grumpy woman, with a litany of complaints, "The corner is so dirty- move the sofa and broom, there is dust on the little table- clean it properly, scrub hard- there are so many stains on the floor..."

At least *Badi Mummy* was pleasant to talk to and always asked about her mother's health, "How's Aruna? What did the doctor say?" Yesterday she had given Jahnvi a banana from her puja thali – (prayer plate) it was a little overripe but at least some parts were edible, and she offered a few wrinkled *mosambis* (sweet lime) for her sick mother. *Aai*

15

managed to suck out some juice from them. But that vulture Badi Bhabhi? She only pointed out mistakes.

Jahnvi went to the kitchen to keep the broom. Now began the loathsome part. She had to wash the utensils while that *Kutta* Vijay cooked the lunch. Most days he would deliberately lean across her and brush against her chest to pick up a utensil or turn off the water filter. Thankfully today the *Kutta* was busy cooking and Badi Bhabhi was barking instructions. "How many times do I have to tell you- 2 spoons of oil only? Can't you see how fat *Badi Mummy* has become? It affects her heart. *Par tumko kya?* (you don't care) You just keep adding oil and butter to everything so it becomes tasty. Tasty my foot. Who will pay the doctor's bill? And oil is also not free, is it?"

Vijay wished he could smash her with the *kadchi* (scoop)and seal her mouth shut. But since that was not a possibility - the Narangs paid him a good sum for his services- he chose the next best option and zoned out, mechanically going along with the cooking and mentally chopping *Badi Bhabhi's* fingers one by one. Jahnvi quickly rinsed the last of the utensils and walked out to mop the living room.

Badi Mummy, as usual, was scrolling through her phone watching videos while the TV blared in the background. She had a big bowl of *makhanas* next to her. While she lazed on the sofa, she popped a few in her mouth every few seconds. Didi walked in with her phone- "*Badi Mummy* look at this." She thrust her phone in front of *Badi Mummy*'s eyes, "Just look at this stupid picture." *Badi Mummy* rolled her eyes. "*Hai*, who is this girl- such big boobs beta. Photoshop *hai*? How can she be so big?"

"*Badi Mummy*," Didi rolled her eyes, you only look at boobs! You are as bad as these creeps!" *Badi Mummy* grinned, "*beta* at least they are visible- not like yours *sookhe kishmish*- how many times I have told you to eat *badaam* and drink a big glass of saffron milk." Jahnvi stifled her laughter! What would Badi Mummy call her own saggy, wrinkled ones? Just then *Badi Bhabhi* walked in, and Didi wailed, "Mom, look at this. That creep Rohan has sent me another vulgar pic on my DM." She pushed the phone under her mother's nose. *Badi Bhabhi* scowled. "Rascal. This is the second time he has done this. Wait, I will call his mother right now. She needs to know what a lousy son she has given birth to."

"No Mom. I have a better idea. I'm going to shame him in public. Let's lodge a police complaint."

"*Paagal ho kya*?" (are you mad) screamed *Badi Mummy*- "*ladke karte hai aisa* (boys do things like this) Let it be. Young guys are like little puppies- they only bark- they don't bite- they don't have the guts." Badi Mummy snatched her phone and hit the delete button, "just ignore. Why go to police-*shulice* and spoil your name? They will ask 1000 questions, force you to file a case, and then those journalists will splash it in newspapers. We don`t want all that."

Didi fumed, "Mom you at least call his mother." She turned towards *Badi Mummy*, "What if I just put out an anonymous tweet or post something on Instagram with the hashtag me too?"

"Enough." *Badi Bhabhi* said harshly. "I will speak to his mother and handle it. You ignore his messages. No need to do all this extra stuff and invite unnecessary trouble."

Badi Mummy dusted her hands, picked up the remote, and changed the channel. "We don`t want to do all this stupidity. If a mad dog barks you don't retaliate. You change your route. So, no need to post anything," she spoke firmly, "and you," she turned towards *Badi Bhabhi*, "don't call the mother. She will defend her son and badmouth our daughter. Just ignore." *Didi`s* shoulders drooped, she picked up her phone and walked back to her room. *Badi Bhabhi* nodded her head in disgust and sank on the sofa.

Jahnvi was puzzled. She followed Didi into the room. "*Didi*, what's hashtag me too? Why is *Badi Mummy* so angry about it?"

Didi gave her a condescending look. "How do I

explain this to you Jaanu? If a man is indecent or says or does some bad things to you then you can write about it and add #metoo. Then you post on social media like X or Insta. This way you shame them and let everyone know you are being harassed. Anyways why am I telling you all this? As if anyone would do that to people like you."

Jhanvi straightened her kurta, "You don't know how many men do that. This cook Vijay, passes dirty comments whenever he sees me alone. He tries to brush against my chest whenever he walks past me. I have an Instagram ID. I will make a post and add the # metoo. Then everyone will know what a creep he is!"

Badi Bhabhi overheard the conversation as she walked into the room. She pounced immediately, "No need to do anything like that. You do your work and ignore Vijay. He's like that only. Just cover your chest decently with your dupatta. Why do you have to tie it to your waist? You want to show yourself off and then you complain. Don't you dare say anything about him! He's a fantastic cook; he manages my kitchen. And here you come for two days and talk rubbish. Tell your mother to come tomorrow. If she can't I will call someone else." *Badi Bhabhi* turned towards Didi. "And you, stop being on the phone the whole day. Why do you have to open every message?

Me too. Me too. Stop focussing on yourself and learn to be smart around these creeps."

Jhanvi timidly walked out of the room. Cleaning this house is tough, she mumbled. Once *Aai* is back on her feet, I will be free. I will post it on my Instagram. Maybe then *Didi* will pluck the courage to do the same.

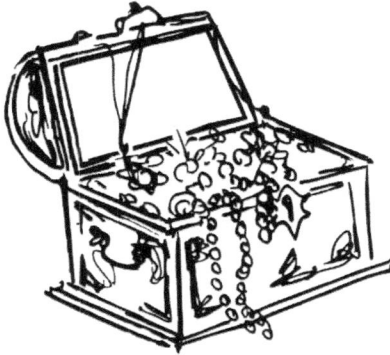

So Nature deals with us, and takes away
Our playthings one by one, and by the hand
Leads us to rest so gently, that we go
Scarce knowing if we wish to go or stay...

H.W.Longfellow

Baanu

Baanu squirmed in her bed. The sun's rays spilled over her pillow and pierced her eyes. She turned her head and tried to move her stiff body to find a darker spot. The clock had not yet struck 9, and the sun had already spread its hot arms and engulfed the room greedily. The sweltering heat almost choked her as the fan whirred slowly, struggling and failing miserably in its attempt to push the balmy air.

She sighed. Her life was a sweaty, dirty mess, and there was no escaping from it. For the umpteenth time, she cursed her strong Parsee genes, which ensured that arthritis, encephalitis, scaly skin, and even diarrhoea for days altogether could not break her body. She wasn't sure if death was the answer to this suffering so she just plodded along. If only her beloved Ferdoon were alive. He went away too soon. Which Parsee worth his salt would die at the age of 67? Ferdoon did, leaving her widowed at 62. The last twenty-five years had been tough. To be honest, maybe the last five years had been a drag. Till she hit the 80 mark, she was in good shape; her spine was ramrod straight, she had a sprightly gait, and a healthy appetite. Things started going downhill after a fall in the bathroom- that good-for-nothing Chanda did not scrub the floors-they were so slippery and that day she was in a rush and... She shuddered every time she thought about it. The sharp pain in her hip flared occasionally as a painful reminder of the evening she slipped into the bathroom and lay for over six hours. Freny, her niece, had found her sprawled in the shower, whimpering incoherently.

Baanu heard someone insert a key in the lock of the door, and it creaked as it opened. "That sly Freny," she muttered. Her ears strained to follow Freny's footsteps as she tip-toed towards the storeroom. A muffled metallic sound as the iron trunk protested softly, and she knew what Freny was up to. "*Badmaash chokri* (wicked girl) is opening my precious trunk again. She thinks I am old, and deaf, and senile, and I won`t get to know? Thief of the first order, she will have to face the music one day -*Pacchi buddhi hove te khabar pavegi,* (she will know when she gets old) how tough it is to feign ignorance when your supposedly loved ones pull a fast one on you," she muttered. In the last few days, Freny had opened the trunk that held Baanu`s precious sarees and shawls at least thrice. Baanu fretted but knew that she had to let it pass- an old, lonely, home-bound widow has no option but to learn to swallow her anger and accept with gratitude whatever little comes her way.

Though Freny had been pilfering away her sarees, shawls, porcelain crockery, linen, and other household knick-knacks, Baanu could not complain. How could she? Living alone was tiresome, and she was thankful that Freny came in every morning and checked on her. Usually, she got Banoo a boiled egg, a banana, and a small glass of milk. Occasionally, she would get a few slices of bread or a sweet *maska* bun. However, for the last week, she had gotten only 2 bananas a day after Baanu had complained of an upset stomach.

Last week's conversation was still fresh in her mind. "Aunty, we have to give your stomach a rest. *Tamey kitti baar bola havey* (how many times have I told you?), don't take anything from these neighbors. You can't be eating all this *pulav* and *samosa* and *dahi bada* and all this junk these people give you. All the leftovers these useless people give you. You are too *seedha*. You think they are nice and kind because they give you food and all." Freny ranted. "Huhh", Baanu protested, "they are nice people. Good neighbors. It's not their fault that I fell sick. It is too hot and maybe I overate the *pulav*. It was so delicious. When you eat something after a long time then ...."

"You have to control yourself. These greedy taste buds of yours are going to land you in big trouble, I am telling you. At this age, you look at food as medicine- eat a small portion, not gobble away mouthfuls," Freny reprimanded her again.

"Hmm. But I am always so hungry. You don't know how much I crave flavours- spicy, hot, sweet, sour...oh the taste of *salli boti, patra-ni- macchi, dhansak, dal gosht,* caramel custard...oh my mouth waters just thinking about them. The other day, that kind Mrs. Sharma sent over a bowl of spicy Chola with bread. It was spicy and tangy, and I couldn't resist. I ate the whole bowl and then the gas. Oh, the night was tough," Baanu trailed.

Freny snapped, "Huh. Kind Mrs. Sharma? A wily woman she is! She is eyeing your house and all your stuff. She will pounce like a vulture once you..."

Baanu spoke sharply. "Nothing like that will happen. She is a pious woman. Besides, I have a will."

"I know you do. By the way, have you updated it recently? You better get it registered. Should I call a lawyer? You will need a witness too." Freny motored, "You must tell me where you have kept it. I am your niece. You have to trust family."

Baanu nearly choked on her banana. Family? Bloody vulture, hovering around, waiting to feast on my dead body! If only I could move around freely, I would have kicked this snake out and bolted the door forever. She sighed. Life was tough at 87. She had to keep her anger in check. She mumbled, "Mr. Sooi had come last week. He said he will do what is needed. I don`t have to worry about it. He has kept the document safely for me."

"Mr. Sooi? Uncle Freddy's friend? When did he come? What did he say?" Frenny eyed her suspiciously and spoke sharply, "You know *na* that he is not family, and he is not your lawyer, and still, you choose to trust him more than your niece? How can you be sure he won`t tamper with the will? At least you should have let me go through it to see if everything was in place."

Baanu knew she had to put an end to this conversation or else Freny would somehow get to the bottom of this 'I have updated my will' theory, and Mr. Sooi's visit she had concocted to escape the incessant volley of words against that kind Mrs. Sharma. She quickly picked up her trump card: dementia. It was time to let it slide in. She looked at Freny with a confused look. "Mr. Sooi? I haven't seen him for ages. I have given the will to Ferdoon. He said he will keep it in his office. He always keeps the documents safely."

Freny was not the kind who gave up easily so she prodded, "But you just said you gave to Mr. Sooi? How could you have given it to Freddy Uncle? He's been gone over 25 years now."

Baanu's lips quivered. "Where has he gone? He was here with me in the morning. He has stepped out to meet someone. I can't remember who."

Freny sighed. Baanu looked confused and lost, and nodded her head, muttering incoherently. There were times she felt sorry for Baanu Aunty. Old age was cruel. But to be fair to herself, she was also not getting any younger. She had her issues to manage; the early onset of Osteoporosis had been tough on her. Somedays she just could not muster the energy to do all that she had on her plate. She was tired of being the caretaker for all the oldies in her family. Admittedly she checked in on Baanu Aunty only 4-5 times a week but she was the one who had the sole responsibility to tend to all the needs of her childless widowed Aunt; call the doctor, arrange for medicines, and food, keep an eye on the lazy maid, and whatnot. Besides Baanu, she also had to look after octogenarian Aunty Sillu and her husband Uncle Jeh. It was not easy being a 45-year-old spinster with no steady income, relying on these oldies to make a provision for her in their will. How much could she manage? She just wanted them to die now. Enough!

**

Baanu tossed helplessly in her bed while waiting for Freny to come in. She didn't want to call out aloud and let Freny know that she was awake and knew exactly what Freny was up to. After an agonizing wait, Freny came in and asked in a chirpy tone, "Good morning, Aunty. How are you? I got you eggs and milk. Should I help you get up? You want to go to the bathroom?"

"How would I ever manage without you? "Baanu smiled gratefully. "You would manage just fine. *Accha* come on, get up now. I have lots to do today," piped Freny. "You know it is Pesi's birthday. I am going to his house in the evening. Do you have a nice saree I could borrow?"

"Pesi? That Siloo's nephew?"

'Yea. I bumped into him when I went to Agiyari (fire temple) the other day. He has a small party at home."

"Hmm. Let me eat something, then I will check

one of the trunks in the storeroom. I may have one that would be just right for you."

"I may have one. Huh! Old witch. Trunks and trunks of clothes, and she claims she may have one. Holding on to everything till she dies. Miser woman, not letting go of her life also. Struggling every day but won't give up." Freny muttered caustically.

"What are you saying, Freny? I can't hear you at all."

"I am just reciting a prayer for you, Aunty. Now come on, hold my hand," Freny replied, "we can't have you falling all the time."

Freny helped her aunt brush her teeth, wiped her face gently, and led her to the dining table. Baanu sat on the chair and peeled the over-ripe banana. The sweet mushiness did not appeal to her palate, but she could not afford to complain or state her preferences. Freny did not take to complaints kindly. She moved on to the hard-boiled egg, sprinkled some salt and pepper over it, and ate small bites, picking the tiniest crumb that fell from her mouth onto her floral nighty. She then sipped on the lukewarm milk, savoring each sip as she knew this could be her only meal of the day unless her kind neighbors remembered to send her some *sabzi* or *daal*. The cook had long disappeared and she had to rely on Freny and her kind neighbours for food. She had biscuits and nuts to munch on, but they hardly left her satisfied. She craved hot, wholesome meals. There were 2 slices of bread, and she wanted to dip them in the milk until they became soft and plump, but she resisted. Better to save the bread for the evening. Maybe that kind Mrs. Sharma would send her a small bowl of vegetables or *daal* in the evening, and then she could tear off small pieces and dunk them into the *daal.*

Baanu could hear Freny humming in the kitchen as she washed the cup, glass, and water jar. Baanu hated this waste of water. Water is precious. You can`t keep the tap running while you sing and soap the dishes. But she couldn't possibly tell that to Freny. The last time she tried telling Freny, she had met with cold silence, and then Freny did not drop by for two days. She still could not forget the painful spasms of hunger that wracked her stomach that evening. It was that kind Mrs. Sharma who had sent her some food, or else she would have died. Well, maybe not died, but yes, definitely she would have starved. Let her waste it, you keep your mouth shut, she scolded her finicky self.

Freny walked in with a steel jar filled with water to the brim. Baanu wanted to tell her that the jar was heavy. Wouldn't it be better if she filled three small bottles and kept them by her bedside and maybe a couple of them on the dining table? She looked at Freny and decided not to say anything. No point in inviting her wrath over such trivial issues!

"Aunty, can we see the saree now?"

"Yes." Banoo burped and farted loudly at the same time.

"Aunty, you are too funny," laughed Freny.

Baanu just nodded and held on tightly to Freny as she slowly dragged her enormous feet. Encephalitis had curbed her movements. She sat heavily on the bed as Freny dragged the trunk from under the bed.

"Aunty, give me the keys".

Baanu removed the thick white string around her neck and handed it to Freny, who made a great show of opening the already broken lock while Baanu looked out of the window. The sun had begun its upward journey, and the room was almost sizzling with heat. "So pretty," Frenny exclaimed as she pulled out a heavy silk saree. She ran her fingers lovingly over the delicate crimson flowers embroidered intricately on the emerald green saree.

Baanu stepped back in time as she dreamily looked at the saree. She had draped this one for the cocktail party at the club. A grand retirement party was hosted in honor of her beloved Freddy, a judge in the Allahabad court. Scores of colleagues, superiors, and juniors had assembled to toast his glorious tenure; the faint tinkling of the glasses and the smooth notes of jazz filled the room. The pearls that Freddy had gotten for their 35th anniversary gleamed as she walked around the room greeting the guests. Aah, those were the days...

Clang! The harsh sound broke her reverie as Freny closed the trunk with a thud and pushed it roughly under the bed. Baanu was disoriented for a minute.

"I need to run now. I will come and see you after three days' now. After the party, we plan to go to Pesi`s sister's house for two days. I will tell Ramesh *panwaala* to check on you every day. He will get you eggs, milk, and bread every day. And don`t give him any money, please. Don`t call for samosa and all roadside food," Freny instructed as she rushed out, clutching onto the saree, leaving Baanu sitting on the bed.

Baanu knew that a saree could only get her this much to ease her life. Maybe it was time to part with sweet memories and start trading them for some tasty meals. She could give her small filigree silver *batua* (purse) to Mrs. Sharma as a Diwali present. That would ensure at least a few weeks of food: bowls of *chola, rajma, paalak* soup, and an occasional *ladoo* or *rabri*. And maybe she would give Freny a birthday gift- her pearl necklace that nestled in a velvet box, hidden behind the old sweaters in her cupboard. Surely, the pearls would fetch her some *Dhansak* and *Patra-ni-Macchi* and maybe some more delicacies for a few days.

Her mouth watered as she began the slow, painful walk back to her room. It was time to pull her life back on track.

I should be happy with my lot:
A wife and mother – is it not
Enough for me to be content?

Elizabeth D.B. Stoddard

Priya

The soft jazz notes filled her heart. Aah, she loved evenings like this. A soft breeze caressed her as she walked barefoot on the grass, humming and picking flowers in her terrace garden. She placed the delicate Shiuli flowers in a crystal bowl filled to the brim with water, walked up to the console, and placed it next to the marble sculpture that Rohit had picked for her from one of his travels to Europe; an exquisitely carved bird ready to take off, "It reminds me of you; always wanting to fly away and explore opportunities," he had whispered. She had loved it. Though she didn't have any opportunities and no open sky either, she thought the idea was charming – fly away and explore.

Her phone buzzed, "Pree, my love you have to, have to, have to come. Sweety, it`s my 40th! I am not taking no for an answer, ok? The whole gang is invited- and listen, I am not inviting The Random Group, only the Soul Sistahs. So not a peep to anyone as of now, ok?" Sabina's husky voice flowed like honey. Priya's heart pumped with excitement. She could barely breathe! Exhilaration seeped in, and Priya chuckled. O.M.G.!!! *The* Sabina was inviting her for her 40th! Never mind that she had a 40th two years back - a huge dance party at Tryst, or was it at Aer? Does it matter how old she's turning- if she says it`s her 40th birthday, then it`s her 40th. Why should I complain? I can`t do that- not when she invites me - that too to Budapest for a 3-day Girls' trip!

Priya couldn't contain her excitement. She had to release it lest she burst. She dialed Ritu, "Ritz you got a call, babe?"

"Yeah! From that Sabina *na*? Such a bitch. I was planning my 40th there this summer. She hijacked the idea." Ritu`s voice dripped with fury. Priya felt deflated. She didn't want to say anything. She was excited about Sabina`s party but couldn't cross swords with Ritu, especially when she had such fancy plans! "Hmm. So now?" murmured Priya. "Now what? We go for *her* party. I am not so petty yaa. I`ll plan something else- not breathing a word about it to anyone now. Ok, I`ll catch you. Have to pick up Shanaya from her piano class." Ritu hung up on her abruptly.

Priya sighed. She was still new to this kitty circuit and continued to tread carefully lest she committed some faux pas. When she joined two kitty party groups three years back after a decade of being a homebound dutiful mother and daughter, a new world opened up for her. Though Mummy derided Kitty party groups and labeled them as a lot of unnecessary *shoo-shaa*, the interactions Priya had with her kitty friends had caused minor explosions in her routine. The last three years had been fun and stressful at the same time. Her phone buzzed constantly thanks to the two WhatsApp groups; Random Group and Soul Sistahs. From memes to music videos to scandalous news to maid problems to mil rants- these conversations added spice to her otherwise mundane life.

Some days, she felt she was constantly walking over an edge, balancing her kitty outings and household responsibilities; it was exhausting, but she didn't want to give it up. Her kitty outings led to more party invites- birthdays, anniversaries, Diwali lunches, Christmas brunches, Holi bashes, etc and her social calendar buzzed during the festive season.

She loved it.

Priya walked out on the terrace and sat on the cane chair next to the Shiuli shrub, gently caressing the petals, breathing in the sweet, floral heady fragrance of the Shiuli flowers. She often wondered why it was called the Tree of Sadness. It bore delicate flowers that bloomed every evening- albeit for a few hours only- filling her with joy, and today, they were merrily dancing with the breeze. Her excitement seemed to have rubbed off, them too. Budapest would be so much, so much fun.

Her mind raced with thoughts and she started making a list of what she would need for the trip- she would definitely buy those tinted aviators. The green ones that she had seen on Instagram. But so many of the Kitty girls had green or blue aviators. Maybe she should go in for gold. She had to be different; she didn't want to be accused of copying someone. And she would need a long jacket- with fur fringe- and maybe a pair of long boots. Thank God she had got her kitty money last month. Rohit would freak out at her shopping list. She could go with Gayatri, her sensible friend who had an eye for fashion, to the mall. Surely, they could find some excellent first copies at one of those boutiques in Bandra.

She nearly jumped out of her skin when she heard

Rohit whisper in her ear, "Preee." She turned around and hugged him. "Oh! sweetheart. I have to tell you something. Sabina called. We are going on a Girls` trip for her 40th."

Rohit asked, "We? We as in?"

Priya gushed, "Our Soul Sistah`s group."

Rohit frowned, "You told Mummy about it or not?"

"No, I haven't. Sabina just called a while back...I thought I would tell you first and then..." Priya`s voice trailed.

"And then what? You know how it goes Pree. After 15 years of marriage, you don`t get it? I don't want to take sides. You fight your own battles. You tell Mummy. And then Dad. I have no issues, you can travel to Timbuktu if you want, but I will not ask for permission or anything. *Chalo* come now. I'm going down to eat. Mummy said dinner at 7:30 today. It's almost 7:15."

Rohit walked away breezily. Priya chewed her lips. Well, Rohit was always happy to inform his parents and accompany her for all the parties and outings planned by the Kitty Groups, but if ever there was a Girls` plan, he refused to talk about it to his parents. Priya had to do the needful, only in this case not inform, but ask before going out. Whenever a sundowner or a drinks-only session was planned, Priya could not muster the courage to tell Mummy about it. Once or twice, she did manage by saying that it was a hi-tea party, but such outings for her were rare. Priya steeled herself. I have to go this time. I mean, what's the big deal? I have my money to spend. I have enough savings from my household expenses and kitty-savings and *kharchis.*(cash gifts) The kids are teenagers- old enough to manage without me for a few days. There are house-helpers for daily chores. Priya mumbled to herself as she walked down to Mummy's apartment.

They ate all their meals with her in-laws. Rohit was sprawled over the sofa, munching chips. Mummy was busy knitting yet another cardigan for Manju, or maybe this one was for Manju's husband Mukund. Mummy was obsessed with Manju. "*Hai meri rani beti-* She is so delicate. *Dilli ki thand-* she cannot bear it." So, every year during monsoons, Mummy would go into this knitting mode churning out cardigans, mufflers, skivvies, gloves, *kaan topies-* all for her delicate darling Manju.

"Mummy," Priya said softly as she sank into the worn-out sofa that always seemed to devour her. She struggled to find a comfortable position.

"*Haan beta.*"

"Mummy you know Sabina na? My friend from Pali Hill."

"Of course, *beta-* I must say she is a big show-off!" Before Priya could interject, Mummy asked, "Where's Ananya? I haven't seen her since evening."

Her fingers continued to knit.

"She's gone to Twisha's house. Rohit will pick her up after dinner. How much she cried; all her friends had planned to spend the night there. She wanted to do the same, but Rohit said no and I also thought she's just 12…" Priya's voice trailed.

"Of course, *beta*," exclaimed Mummy. "You did the right thing. I don't like this stayover business. She is a girl. It's not safe for her I tell you. But I agree she needs to go out. She can go for dinners and all, but at night? Never. No stayover and all. And you need to stop pushing her so much. How much she studies and then you send her for tuition classes also. I never sent Rohit or Manju for any classes- *vlasses*. And they did well, didn't they? *Nanhi jaan* how much can she do? And then that piano class. *Kahan bajayegi*? (where will she play?) I tell you, Priya, you must not let these *shoo-sha* kitty friends of yours dictate your choices. We are not like them."

Priya could see the conversation going downhill and tried to salvage the situation by turning the conversation towards Mummy's frenemy "Mummy, how's Savita *Behenji*? Is she better now?"

Mummy inspected the cardigan and replied, "Yes, she is a little better. I mean how much better can you feel once you get diabetes? I tell you she never took care. *Jalebi par Jalebi,* she popped when Radha *behen ji* had *satsang* in her house."

Rohit turned and winked at Priya. 'Pree, what

were you saying about Sabina…"

"Haan Mummy," Priya blurted before Mummy could start with another rant. "Sabina has invited me to Budapest for her birthday. I can go *na*?"

"Yes, *beta* go. Do I ever say no for a party? I am not like that Radha who sits like a vulture- eyeing every move of her poor daughter-in-law."

"Mummy you know where's Budapest?" asked Rohit with a smile. "It is a city in Hungary- in Europe."

"Europe? London *ke paas*?" Mummy`s eyebrows shot up. "I thought Budapest was the name of some club. *Aaye Haye beta*, only women without their families? How can you go? You have kids and a family. *Ab tumhari umar nahi hai* (doesn't befit your age) for all this. Anyways, who goes to a foreign country for a birthday party? *Chonchley hai sab.* (Foolish behaviour)"

"Mummy all my friends are going. We are a big group." Priya instinctively knew that this was not going to go her way. But she had to try. After all, it was a trip to Budapest.

"*Beta London se aage*? You know the expense?" Mummyji`s fingers knitted furiously.

"Mummy I just got my kitty…" Priya almost whined.

"*Aaye haye toh uda dogi saari kitty?* (You will spend it all?) Money is for saving. My mother always said money saved is money earned. These trips are not for us. All these fanciful things – a waste of money it is, I am telling you. Useless women. They don't care about their family. *Beta tumhe shobha nahi deta ye sab.* Ramu *khaana laga.*" Mummy ended the conversation firmly. A wave of anger, frustration, and pain welled inside her. She looked at Rohit imploringly. He just shrugged his shoulders. Tough luck he mouthed and walked up to the dinner table just as Daddy came in and sat.

Mummy took her position on his right and poured dal in a bowl for him. "Remember the exhibition we organized at the club last month? Our Mahila Mandal raised Rs.250,000 for the renovation of *Mata* temple!" Daddy nodded while she served him a hot *chapati,* "Really? That's commendable Shobha. You all should raise money for other charitable events also." Mummy beamed with pleasure. "We will save some money after all the expenses. So, Sarita *Behenji* suggested that we should go on a pilgrimage to thank Sai Baba. We will go to Shirdi. She will hire a bus. It's a day trip, but Radha *Behenji* was saying that *Kakad Aarti* is the best, so we will stay one night. You know there's a nice guest house near the…"

"Shobha!" interrupted Daddy. "What is the need? Why do you have to go to Shirdi to thank Baba? You can thank him right here. *Baba humare dil main hai*(Baba lives in our hearts). *Chonchley hai sab.*

Wastage of money. Useless women. They don't care about their family. *Ab tumhari umar nahi hai* for all this. You have to be mindful of your health." He turned to Rohit and asked, "Rohit, where's Arav?" Priya served some *daal* to Rohit as he turned towards his father, "Dad, I told you last week about his plan. It`s Abhay`s 14th birthday. All his close friends have gone to Lonavala- they will stay the night at Abhay`s bungalow. The caretaker is there."

"Hmm" grumbled Daddy. "Priya *beta*, have you made some *meetha* today? Shobha, why aren't you eating?"

"I am", Mummy said softly. The anger and frustration ebbed away from Priya and a wave of sorrow washed over her as she looked at Mummy picking her food listlessly. Their eyes locked momentarily. A stoic silence veiled the pain.

Priya went back to her room after dinner. She tapped on to the 'Best of Jazz' on Spotify and soon melancholic notes filled the room. She walked up to the console, her shoulders drooped- the Shiuli in the bowl had wilted.

True hearts have ears and eyes, no tongues to speak;
They hear and see, and sigh, and then they break.

Edward Dyer

Indu

Indu, *Aiiii* Induuu, are you ready or not? It's nearly 5. They will be here soon. I have kept that pink saree out for you. Wash your face with Lux and get ready fast", shouted Maya from the kitchen.

Indu sighed. The pink saree was laid neatly on the back of the wooden chair in her room, freshly ironed by Mishti. She spotted her high-heeled sandals beside the chair. "This definitely has to be that irritating Mishti's handiwork only," muttered Indu as she snuggled inside her bed, folding the soft *dohar* all around herself. She opened her diary and gently held up the thick creamy paper tucked inside it. Her name was artfully cut out on the paper and two hand-painted pink flowers adorned the corners. She flipped through the diary, full of cut-outs of her name on thick and creamy card papers; a few were done on marble paper. A sketch accompanied each cut-out; a dove, a butterfly, a swan, a dragonfly, a cat. Pink, blue, yellow, red, green, violet- all the colours of the rainbow were there and each coloured paper had her name Indu cut out in different fonts, and sizes-one even had her name written in Hinglish.:ṇndu.

Indu caressed the papers as her thoughts flew to D'Souza. His table was just across from hers in the Shakti Bhawan; the electricity department of their city, where they both worked as clerks. Most days they could not see each other, thanks to the mountain of paperwork on their tables, but during lunch hours, when they both walked up to the canteen, they managed to steal a few glances at each other. Their conversations were limited to a few thank yous, good mornings and how are yous. Some days when she would go to the water cooler to refill her water bottle, D`souza would follow- mind you, only once in a while- to refill his bottle too. Though the meeting at the cooler was rare, it was full of excitement for her. D'Souza would invariably empty his bottle and make a great show of rinsing his bottle again and again and she did the same. They hardly exchanged words or smiles, but the chemistry between them was palpable.

This scenario had been played out five times in

the last month. Since last week though Indu had been avoiding this rendezvous lest she fall prey to office gossip like that Rita, from the Accounts department on the 3rd floor, had. Every day Rita would drop by on their floor on the pretext of dropping or picking up some document, discussing something urgent or reporting something scandalous to Asha, who sat diagonally opposite Verma. Verma would wink at Rita or crack a joke at her expense and Rita would pretend to be annoyed. But that didn`t stop her from dropping by daily and the whole floor spoke in hushed tones about Rita and Verma- and her antics to attract his attention. She didn`t want to be the next Rita. No way. Definitely, not Rita! She had to maintain the distance to keep the gossip at bay. So, she stepped away from her desk only during lunch hour and went to the canteen with two other clerks on her floor.

A few months back, one day when she reached her desk after lunch, she found an intricate cut-out of her name on coloured paper carefully placed under her pile of files. She called out to the peon, "Shankar, who has kept this here? He shrugged his shoulders "I didn`t see anyone. Ask D`Souza Sir. He kept some files on your desk." She turned to look at D`Souza who looked steadfastly at the file on his desk and refused to meet her eye. She was bewildered and didn't know what to make out of it. But it was a pretty cut-out! She slid open her drawer and placed the paper carefully inside it. Since then, every Monday, post-lunch a coloured paper with a cut out of her name was neatly placed under the files on her table. She would pick it up, smile, trace her fingers across it, and safely tuck it in her drawer.

One day she got a diary, tucked all the cut-outs in, and took them home. Her favourite weekend pastime now was to spread all the cut-outs on her bed, trace her name, and hum along to the songs playing on the radio in the background. She loved it all! The paper cut-outs and the songs. Though she never saw D`Souza place them nor had he ever said anything to her, she had seen him making similar cutouts- of flowers and animals on days when *Bade Babu* (senior clerk)was not around. He didn't give these artistic offerings to anyone else. No one received these cut-outs ever and she was sure he liked her- why else would he painstakingly draw out only her name on delicate paper? Agreed, her name was easy to spell- and write on paper and cut- it hardly had any curves, just like her body, but maybe, just maybe, he liked her?

"Indu. *Ae* Indu." Her mother`s shrill call broke her reverie. Indu gently placed the papers back in her diary and sighed, "Yes, Ma. Give me 10 minutes." She better get ready before Ma sent her spy, Mishti to see what was keeping her away. Mishti was a pain. She would run and report everything to Ma- everything spiced with her own opinions, "Didi was again just smiling at some papers, and singing, and looking out of the window. *Maashi,* you really need to take her to Bengali baba at the chowk. Someone has cast a spell on her, I tell you. Full day Didi just smiles or looks up at the ceiling and hums."

Indu washed her face with Lux as per her mother's instructions, squeezed a big blob of boroline cream on her palm and rubbed it on her face vigorously. She draped the crisp cotton saree, carefully pinned the pallu on her shoulder, and examined herself critically in the small mirror on her wooden dressing table. Thankfully, she was lean: all angles, no unsightly curves or bulges. Actually, she was not bad to look at quite ok. Only if her complexion was better. After 200 tubes of Fair & Lovely and *katoris* and *katoris* of *besan* and *malai ubtan* she had given up on her quest for fair skin. Enough. If God had decided she should have a dusky complexion, then so be it.

She lined her eyes with a thin line of *kajal* and stuck the small maroon *bindi* between her thick brows. She plaited her hair neatly, letting it fall heavily on her waist as she wore the tiny *jhumkas* reserved for such viewings. Ma said they added a sparkle to her face. Unfortunately, no prospective groom had so far agreed with Ma. She slipped the thin gold chain around her neck and dabbed a little rose *ittar* on her wrists and behind her ears. She picked up the lipstick and hesitated. She looked at her diary with the cut-outs peeping and decided to let the lipstick be and rubbed her lips with Vaseline.

"Didi, come on now *Maashi* is calling you. Fast. The groom is already here. He`s quite fair you know and…" Mishti went on hastily as she snuck a handkerchief into Indu`s hand.

'You go Mishti. I will just come."

"No Didi. *Maashi* said I have to get you. Come now. No smiling and singing now."

Indu wanted to slap Mishti. Always breathing down her neck, spying on her, and reporting unnecessary details to Ma. She wished the prospective groom who had come for viewing would say yes to the proposal, just so that she could escape this annoying midget!

She went down with Mishti and headed to the kitchen. The tray was already laid out with different plates of tiny samosas, biscuits, *chivda*, and a small plate of *laddu*. Indu picked up the tray while Mishti carried another tray with a plump teapot draped in a bright yellow tea cosy - the deep red flowers Indu had embroidered on it last month stood out. Ma made sure that Indu spent her weekends doing embroidery, painting or crocheting. After all, she needed proof that her daughter was *sarvagun sampan* (all-rounder). Indu enjoyed working with her hands, and in the last few years had churned out embroidered tablemats, napkins, table cloths, handkerchiefs with delicate scalloped lace and even a small scenery that was now framed and displayed in the drawing room. She had hand-painted a couple of sarees and a bedsheet but they were tough to display. Ma managed to somehow weave these accomplishments into her conversations with any and everyone who asked anything about Indu.

Indu entered the drawing room and Ma smiled broadly "Indu. Come *beta*, sit next to me," and then she rapidly went on, "This is my Indu. Very talented girl. She takes care of everything. Since her father passed away three years back, she has been managing everything. She has a government job in Shakti Bhavan, she cooks, sews, embroiders, takes care of taxes, and manages banking…" Ma went on and on but all Indu could hear was the desperation in her voice. The fear of rejection from prospective grooms weighed heavily on Ma and she tried to cover it with her incessant listing of Indu`s achievements. This was Indu`s 17th viewing and she was still single. Indu knew that Ma could not take another no. It would kill her faint heart.

She picked up the teapot and poured tea into the floral cups. Her muscle memory ensured that she did not fill the cups to the brim while her mind continued with a parallel conversation- she`s great at managing but has a dark complexion, and she is 29. Now, that is tough to overlook- throw in the fact that she won't bring a fat dowry, and it`s now an insurmountable task to find her a groom.

Indu picked up the tea cups and offered them to the guest- her eyes looking out for the boy. But there was no boy. Only an old lady and a plump middle-aged man who looked hungrily at the samosa sat across her.

"Kaisi ho?" the old lady asked while she looked at Indu`s face critically as she took the cup. "Anil, you want to ask her anything?"

"No *Ma*. You see and ask. You have to live with her and manage. I have my things to do in life, and if she works for you, she works for me." He took a long sip of the tea and popped a samosa in his mouth. He turned and looked at Indu. "I am hardly home. I am a senior member of the workers' union and hardly get time for myself. Even on Sundays, I have meetings. I don`t have time for movies, shopping, and other stuff. We go ahead with this only if you are Ok with that."

"Well, all men are busy; they have to work. Indu

knows that. Even her father was out most of the time." Ma looked at Indu imploringly. Indu nodded. The old lady retorted, "Anil is a big man in his office. So busy that he has no time even for himself. Why else would a boy who earns a fat salary and comes from a well-known family remain unmarried till the age of 35?"

Anil grinned and shook his head. "Now you both sort it out."

The old lady straightened up and took charge "Indu, you can continue with your job and the housework is not much. It`s just me and Anil and he`s out most days working with the Union workers. I don't want you to leave your job. You can apply for a transfer to Kanpur. Government jobs are not easy to come by. We have very simple meals. Anil rarely eats at home. Only on Sundays do we go a little extra and have an elaborate meal. There is a maid to help with cleaning and washing- she's fairly regular. So, it should be alright. Do you have any questions?"

Indu looked at her mother, who had almost collapsed with relief. "Indu is very efficient. She manages everything here also.' She picked up a laddu and offered it to Anil. 'She won`t give you any reason to complain.' Anil gobbled the *laddu* and grunted.

The old lady got up and slid a thin gold bangle into Indu's arms. Anil popped another samosa in his mouth. She forced a smile as Ma hugged her tearfully. Romance was good on paper, but had little use in day-to-day life. It was time to lock the diary in a deep recess of her cupboard.

By the high verandah pillars, by the rotting
bloodwood gates,
Crowded town or dreary seaboard, everywhere
some woman waits

Mabel Forrest

MRS. SAXENA

Come, come. I haven't seen you since Sunday. I know, it's a new neighbourhood and it takes time to settle. You have been here now for more than a week? Do you need sugar or have you run out of milk again? Oh! you want tomatoes! Open the fridge, you can take some from the top shelf there. Take 4-5. Mr. Saxena got 2 kgs just yesterday.

Oh no! Again, the cable connection is gone. This cable guy Pandey I tell you- number one *haraami*! He charges for three months at a go- full 2250 rupees, mind you- but there's no connection half the time.

And now he doesn't even show that channel of Pakistani serials. *Hai Ram* such pretty girls in these serials I tell you. So soft spoken, so well dressed, and have you seen their skin? Glowing like stars, I tell you, and such pink lips. These Lahoris I tell you-*khoon bada lal hai inka.* (they are red-blooded) And look at my Pinky. The only thing pink about her is her name! What to say? Doctors say that children get equal parts from their parents but Pinky seems to have got everything from my husband Mr. Saxena-both his complexion and his surly nature.

Well, what to say about him now? His entire *khandaan* appears to have been eating baingan for generations! That's why their skin is…*khair, ab kya karein?* (Now what can we do?) I don't know why my Amma was blown by Mr. Saxena and his *khandaan.* Ok, granted he was an engineer in PWD - *sarkari* Naukri (government job) and all and he had his own scooter and was based in Lucknow but then I was no less! A graduate in 1964- mind you that too from BHU- fair, tall, and well, ok, a little plump. But I was a beauty by most standards.

Amma was very liberal- she sent me and my sister Chitra to university, and she ensured we took music lessons, and rode bicycles, though of course she did put us through endless embroidery, sewing, knitting, and cooking classes but she also let us read lots of

books. Have you read Mahadevi Varma? Or
Maithilli Sharan Gupt? *Sakhi wo mujhse kehkar
jaate*....aaah what a poem! The way he has captured
Yashodhra. You know who she is *na*? You people
don`t read literature I tell you. My mother was very
strict and we couldn't be caught reading magazines
and all- only Dharam Yug was allowed you see. And
of course, she wanted us to get married to someone
from a professional background, so Chitra got
married to Dr. Sarkar, a Bengali doctor in our
neighborhood. Amma was above all these castes-
sub-caste issues as long as one was Hindu, it was
fine. You see when a distant cousin suggested Mr.
Saxena, a Kayastha boy for me, a Brahmin, she
wasn't flustered at all. "As long as the boy is good
the caste doesn't matter," she had declared.

But what did Amma know? She couldn't foresee
my future, could she? She had no control over my
destiny- well little maybe- after all, she chose Mr.
Saxena. He had a lot of attitude when we got married,
I tell you- you don't believe me? *Arrey* this man you
see sitting quietly on the veranda reading paper the
whole day, was once an aggressive man with a loud
booming voice. Most evenings he would stride in the
house like a lion-fuming over some altercation at
work and scream at us for the smallest of things. You
know for many years he would just toss the plate with
the rice *daal- sabzi* if I forgot to keep a green chili on

the side. Such a temper I tell you. My children would scurry like mice when they heard his scooter puttering away and entering the lane. Munna *toh* never looked into Mr. Saxena's eyes- to be fair neither did Gudiya or Pinky.

Gudiya! *Arrey* that's my elder daughter. She was here for two weeks and she left just last week. She lives in Canada now with her husband. No kids she has. She tells me they are a nuisance, she claims *jhanjhat hai phaltu ka*! (Unnecessary issue) She is very bold. She even talks to Mr. Saxena directly, and looks into his eyes- in fact, this time she gave it back to him, "Papa why do you harass mummy? Can you not tell the *Aayah* to make breakfast for you? And why do you need to eat breakfast at exactly 8 a.m.?" Mr. Saxena was so taken aback, that he didn`t utter a word. He did mumble under his breath though.

Do you know Mr. Saxena lives by the clock? 8 a.m. breakfast- 2 hard-boiled eggs, 1 slice of toast, 1 apple, and a cup of tea with a teaspoon of sugar. He thinks he's some Englishman! He wants lunch at 12.30 p.m. every day. Whether he's hungry or not- he will eat. Dal, rice *sookhi sabzi*, green chili, and curd. Really a creature of habit I tell you. He drives me crazy. Chana dal is not good for him- he keeps farting the whole day. But *na ji* Thursday is supposed to be the day for *chana daal* and *chana daal* is what he will eat every Thursday. Then evening 4:30 p.m. he wants tea with 2 Marie biscuits. 6 p.m. a bowl of namkeen. Dinner 7:30…I can`t go on with his routine! It's exhausting to live by the clock like this I tell you.

I complained to my son Munna when he came in the summer to see us. He comes every year- not that London is very far but you see he doesn`t get a leave easily. When you become a big *Sahab* it's not easy I tell you. His wife Veena, she doesn't come. She came three years back. She has a mind of her own. Mr. Saxena just cannot stand her. He says that she has no manners - no etiquette. So, I was telling you that I complained to Munna. Mr. Saxena keeps on hoarding all these flyers that come in the newspapers. Every single scrap of those leaflets that come with the newspaper- pressure cooker repair shop, to heavy discount on silk sarees, to free eye check-ups at Balrampur- the man just hoards these flyers. Munna lost it that day when he walked into Mr. Saxena`s room, "Papa why do you make so much of a mess- *kabaad khana bana rakha hai!"* (you have made it a wasteyard) He threw out all the flyers and you know what, Mr. Saxena didn't say a word! Can you imagine- he just sat there and looked while Munna collected mounds of paper and gave them to the *kabadiwala?* And if I dare to tell him about all the mess in his room, he mutters, and mumbles, and sulks for days. Sometimes I think it was better when he screamed and threw things about but then…

Pinky, my younger one, wants to visit us next month. I haven't told Mr. Saxena yet. He doesn't like anyone coming over. His routine goes crazy, he says. Well, he carries on with his timetable, so I don't know how his routine gets disturbed. Every morning at 9 a.m., he fills the plastic buckets and the big plastic tub with water. He is so meticulous, I tell you- filling up everything, every day- from the big plastic tub to small bottles we keep in the fridge, to big *pateelas* in the kitchen, in fact, some days he even fills up all the glasses in the kitchen. You see fresh water from the municipality comes only in the morning. Our house looks like those refugee camps- but it's ok. We need water and it gives him something to do. How much can one read? One newspaper has only that much written in it, isn`t it? He doesn't want to watch T.V. At least I see different shows, songs, and movies on T.V. It's timepass no? But no, he will not see. T.V. He will just sit and read and go and shout at the cycle and scooter *wala`s* when they park outside our gate.

I like to see that Baba Ramdev *ka* channel now. Such good *pranayamas* (Breathing exercises). You know my breathing has improved so much after I have started following his teachings. Mr. Saxena gives me strange looks every time I do the *pranayamas*. We hardly talk to each other now, you see. What is there to talk really? He has his newspaper and the flyers and I have my TV and serials. I make breakfast in the morning. Lunch and Dinner that *Ayah* makes. Her food is not tasty at all, sometimes, he complains and tells me that I should get back to cooking. But I don`t want to. What to cook for two people? I get tired. That newspaper man gets magazines for me, but I just don't like reading anymore.

Arrey, there the cable connection is back. Yes, I know you have to leave. *Aa jaya karo*. It`s nice to see people. Tell your husband also to come. Maybe next time when you come, I will make tea for you. You closed the fridge properly *na*?

She cherished her solitude and didn't want to speak to many,
but as a normal human being she, craved a kind and caring ally.

Solitary Scribble

Geeta Bua

eeta Bua, *kaisi ho*? (how are you?) Mahesh has booked your ticket. He was saying that he wants to see you- we all are missing you. It's been so long since we ate your delicious *besan laddus*. Come fast now."

Geeta beamed with pleasure as she heard Reema speaking rapidly at the other end. She clung to the cell phone, and turned down the volume on the transistor that crooned, "...*ye hai bombay meri jaan,* while she continued folding samosas. Her hands did not know how to rest- they were always busy; cooking, rolling chapatis, folding samosas and *gujhiyas*, or shaping *laddus*.

"Reema I will get them for him when I come. One big dabba (box)only for Mahesh."

"*Arrey nahi,* Geeta Bua, you make them when you come here to stay with us. This time we are not letting you go for at least six months. I am telling you now only. So, don't make any plans ok?" A warm feeling embraced Geeta and she chuckled, "ok baba, ok, I won't make any plans. When do you want me to come? Do you want anything from Jaipur? *Kachori le ayu*? (should I get kachori?) You like them *na*?"

"No no, Geeta Bua nothing. We just want you to come and stay with us for a few months. Then you can make for us all our favourites; *kachori, laddu* and *haan* the *karonde ka achaar*-my mouth is already watering! Come fast now. We have booked you on Aravalli Express for next Thursday. I will send your tickets on the phone. Mahesh will come to receive you, *Accha* Geeta Bua *Pranaam.*"

Geeta did not get a chance to say more as Reema hung up abruptly. Geeta picked up the plate full of samosas and walked towards the kitchen with a spring in her step. Mahesh was her favourite nephew. Mahesh's dad, Brijesh, was her first cousin. She didn't care much for Brijesh but Mahesh was a darling. He loved her cooking, he loved the sweaters she knitted for him, he loved the *champi* (head massage) she gave him, and most of all he loved her. He was always grateful for her care and she loved that about him. She placed the samosas carefully in a big plastic box and sealed it before putting it in the deep freezer. "Second batch done," she mumbled, "one more to go." The deep freezer was already lined neatly with six boxes of shelled peas, and two boxes of spring rolls. She still had to make the *gobhi-shalgam achaar* (cauliflower and turnip pickle) for this season.

"Geeta Bua," she heard Neha calling out, "please come to my room for a minute." Neha was her grand-niece. Her maternal Aunt's granddaughter. Geeta walked into Neha's bedroom and saw her arranging the wardrobe. She sat on the bed and started folding the clothes that were strewn all over the bed. "Yes, *beta*."

"Geeta Bua, I have to go to New York for two weeks." Neha pulled out a jacket and some warm clothes and handed them to Geeta to fold. "I am leaving this Sunday. I have told the cook, and the driver, no *chutti* (leave) for them till I am back. Raj will be back from his work trip by next weekend. I will leave some cash with you for essentials. Please see that Aaira doesn't miss her piano and ballet classes. You know I'm paying through my nose for them. I will call every day so it should be ok. Just be around till the cook and the maid finish and leave.

Then you can go to the garden or wherever you feel like." Neha went on with her instructions.

"But *beta,*" Geeta interrupted, "I am going to Mumbai next Thursday."

"What? Neha`s eyebrows shot up and she frowned, "Mumbai? Why? How can you leave? You didn't tell me about this plan. How can you leave me in a lurch? Who will look after Aaira? When did you decide? What work do you have in Mumbai?" Neha threw a volley of questions at her. Without waiting for Geeta`s response she went on, "Surely you can stay here for another 2 weeks? I had thought you would be here till Aaira's summer vacations begin."

Geeta stumbled, "*Beta* I don't mind staying till then but Mahesh has already booked my tickets and wants me to stay with him for six months. Reema just called and…"

Neha cut her off, "Mahesh wants you to stay? Or is it that sly Reema? Bua these people are very smart. They know how to use you. Of course, they want you there. Reema's daughter-in-law is expecting. They need help during the delivery *na*. You will take care of them, cook and clean, and care for the baby. Bua, *bahut bholi ho tum* (you are so naïve) Do you even know why they love you? It is because you work from them; they get free service, they save money, and they don't have to hire a maid. There's someone responsible for running the show for them. Bua keep away from these poisonous snakes. Just tell her you can`t come. I won`t let you go."

Geeta kept mum. She helped Neha pack and slowly trudged back to her room. Well at least for the duration that she stayed with Neha, the tiny utility room next to the kitchen was 'her' room. It wore a desolate look; bare walls, a calendar hanging on a nail, and a foldable iron board that stood in a corner, adjacent to a tall wooden cupboard. A single bed by the barred window with dull grey curtains was her comfort place and next to it was a small chest of drawers that held her life's fortunes: a few cotton sarees, a pink chiffon saree, that her husband Shyam had bought for her from Mumbai, wrapped in a *mul* cloth, a round wooden box with two thin gold rings, a pair of gold *balis*, a thick *mangalsutra*, a small bronze idol of *Laddu Gopal*, a faded picture of her as a young bride, a passport picture of Shyam- this was all she possessed, besides, of course, a host of memories of her life with Shyam.

She sat by the window as tears welled up in her eyes threatening to wet her cheeks. Her head was swarming with thoughts and she tried to push them away. But they kept surfacing- why did Shyam have to die? She was so angry with him for leaving her in a lurch. Shyam and Geeta lived as a couple for twelve years, before he lost his life to a hit-and-run accident, leaving her childless and almost penniless nearly twenty-eight years ago. Since then, she had been shuffling from one sibling to another, from one nephew to another niece, from one cousin to another, but she never complained. Whoever needed help, called her and she was happy to be of help. It gave her a purpose in life, she felt loved and wanted. What else do you need in life? She had food- good food mind you- and shelter. She was treated as family; eating at the same table, and using the same utensils-even if it was after everyone had finished their meals. So what? She had no home of her own- but she had multiple homes where she was welcomed. She would have to do something; some work to survive. So why not take care of her extended family? This way, she kept her dignity intact, and they in turn took care of her needs. Life was tough for an uneducated widow with no immediate family. At least she was better off than her distant cousin Neelu, who was also a childless widow, and now lived alone in penury.

Geeta wiped her tears. Enough. She couldn`t let misery overwhelm her. There was lots in life to be grateful for she told herself sternly. Neha had bought her two sarees just last month and had told her that this Diwali she would also buy her a gold chain. Geeta picked up her phone and called Mahesh. *"Beta* can you postpone my ticket? I will come after two weeks."

"Why Geeta Bua? You don't love us anymore?' Mahesh teased her playfully.

"Na *beta*. Just this time- please extend by 2 weeks. I will definitely reach before bahu delivers. Neha has to…"

"Geeta Bua," interrupted Mahesh. "Let's not talk about that thankless Neha. Is she troubling you? Forcing you to do her *chaakri*? You keep away from her Geeta Bua. She`s a poisonous snake I am telling you."

"Nahi *beta*, nothing like that- I have to finish a few things, and I promise I will stay for six months- or till whatever time you say."

"Geeta Bua, either you come on Thursday or we look at other options- I can't guarantee anything if you insist on coming late. Reema is very worried. We have to make arrangements before the baby arrives." Mahesh said curtly and hung up.

Geeta held on to the phone, expecting Reema or Mahesh to call her back and assure her that she could take her time. Surely, they would remember how lovingly she had tended to their daughter when she had delivered? She had stayed with them for nearly six months even then. The phone did not ring again.

"Geeta Bua" called Neha, "come here."

"Haan *beta*, coming,"

Geeta walked back to the room again. She knew

she would have to choose between the two soon. Neha or Mahesh?   Where did she have better chances? The transistor played softly, "*Yahan kaun hai tera musafir jayega...*"

A

What's in a name?

That which we call a rose by any other name

would smell as sweet.

William Shakespeare

Bhavna

The air conditioner hummed while the TV droned in the background. It was a sultry day. Her wedding was just five weeks away, and the to-do list seemed never-ending. Bhavna curled on the bed, her mind whirring with a thousand thoughts. There were a zillion things lined up in the next few days: negotiating with the celebrity makeup artist, finalizing a *mehendi* artist, zeroing down on *haldi* party favors, coordinating outfit trials, and to top it all off, now this name business! There was so much to do, yet she didn't feel like venturing out to tick off any tasks from her list. But surely, she could come up with a name without stepping out of the comfort of her room?

Vikas had casually weaved it into his conversation with her last week. "Babes, your name will change after our wedding."

She replied, "Of course, it will. It changes for all girls once they get married. What's the big deal? I will add your surname after my marital name. I will be Bhavna Singh Chadha."

"Well, I am ok with that" he had interrupted, "but your first name will change too. That's the custom in my family. After all, you are stepping into a new role, and a new family so a new name will be apt. *Panditji* suggested that we pick a name with the letter **A**. Do you like any particular name with that letter? You can share 2-3 names, and then we can all decide."

She was taken aback, and it did take her a couple of days to make peace with this new information, but now she was looking forward to the name change. She had never really liked her name. Whoever said what's in a name, obviously wasn't saddled with a humdrum name like Bhavna. It was so ordinary, so meh. Some friends in college had dared to call her Bhavs but had dropped it once they realized she refused to respond it.

The new age names: Shanaya, Riyaana, Diara, Nysa were so cool but she had learned to live with Bhavna. She had long accepted that she didn't have to like her name. Did anyone in this world ever like their name? Parents, relatives, and family astrologers pick a name, and you have to live with it your whole life. No matter how much you dislike it. But at least now she was getting an opportunity to change it. And change as per her choice. How liberating! Your life, your choice, your name. She chose to look at this bright side of it and went ahead with the proposition of changing her name after her wedding. But picking a name was not an easy job. When it came to finalizing one for herself, she found problems with almost all suggestions.

She kicked Reena, her younger sister who was glued to her phone. "Lazybones. Stop scrolling and start looking for a name for me."

"I am," Reena mumbled while gobbling a piece of cake, "that's exactly what I am doing on Instagram. Looking at all accounts and reading their usernames. See look at this one *Di*. Astha What's your take on Astha? It means devotion. Suits you- you are so devoted to Vikki *Jiju* and his family."

"Pleeeease. Stop it already" Bhavna snapped.

"Ok, how about Aishwarya?"

"Too long."

"Anvi?"

"Too short."

"Oh God *Di*! You are so difficult." Reena let out a long sigh.

Bhavna snapped, "Listen, you don't want to help me then just say so, ok? I am not going to settle for any name just because you can't think of a cool one! This is my opportunity to come back with a new identity. Can you imagine- choose my name...I mean how liberating is that? I don't have to be Bhavna anymore. I can be whoever I choose to be."

Reena was puzzled, "But *Di* who is stopping you from being who you choose to be? Just by changing your name, you won't become a different person, will you?"

"Of course, I will. Names have a planetary influence on you. They affect your energies, your persona, your impact..." Bhavna rambled on, "Imagine people calling me Myrah or Raina. I would be so, so stylish and cool."

"*Di* please yaar. Myrah is just a fancy version of Meera and Raina is a twisted Reena. I don't understand why you are so hung up about the name. Chill, it's just a name! Nothing is going to change. You will remain my *Di* irrespective" Reena dusted the cake crumbs off her jeans and got up. She walked over to the bookshelf and picked out a book randomly, "Why don't we just pick up a book and the first name we see you can take that as your new name? What say? Fun *na*?"

Bhavna threw a cushion at her sister and growled,

"Stop this madness. This is not some game we are playing, ok? The first name we see… Idiot. You won`t ever understand why it matters so much to me-you never were Bhavna, so stop trying to make sense of it and google a few more names beginning with A."

"Why only A? Don`t be so stuck-up *Di*. We can look at other alphabets too *na*? You just drooled over Myrah and Raina," Reena pouted.

Bhavna controlled a sarcastic comeback, and took a long breath, "No, we can`t look at just any alphabet. Vikas said their Panditji has given strict instructions that the bride`s name has to start with the alphabet **A**. The stars will be perfectly aligned with Vikas for a happy marriage if the bride`s name begins with A."

Reena piped, "So your stars are not aligned *abhi*? Then how come you both have been dating for over three years? And remind me why are you marrying him?"

Bhavna`s brows knitted with irritation and she scowled, "They are aligned, but once I change my name, the vibrations will be better."

Reena rolled her eyes, "Whatever."

Bhavna went on, "*Panditji* suggested because just like in our community, Vikas`s community also follows the custom of picking a new name for the bride to symbolize the new identity that she adopts to fit into her role as a wife and daughter-in-law. It's almost like taking a new birth. Look around, all the women in our family have done that. Even Ma did it. Everyone calls her Deepa- that was the name given to her after she married Pa but all her school friends and maternal side family call her Rekha *na*. It's a tradition, and so as per this tradition, my name will change too. After all, I am going to be a new person once I marry Vikas. And the vibrations will align to ensure a happy married life. Now you get it? *Chalo* look for some names now."

Reena picked up her laptop again and sank into the bed "*Di*, what rubbish *yaar*. Just by changing your name, you can ensure a happy married life. I mean really? Which world are you living in? And why will you be a new person after marriage? Why can't you be just you? And if you will change then what about Vikki *Jiju*? Are you saying he will change as a person too to align with this new you? If he's going to change, then are you sure you want to be with him? Aaargh! This is so dumb."

Bhavna was irritated, "I don't need your *gyaan* ok. Help if you want to, else just go. I will choose my name and then be whoever I want to be. It's so nice of Vikas to actually ask me to come up with a name I like. His Mom had apparently decided on Anita. Grrr So 80's and 90's *na*? Vikas also said he doesn't want such an old-fashioned name for his wife. Thankfully his family is as liberal as he is. I mean they are letting me choose a name for myself. Who does that?"

Reena smirked and nodded her head as she googled, 'Modern names for Indian girls'. "Well, if that's what you want from life then so be it! What about Archana? Then everyone can call you Archie- that's like so in. It has a nice ring to it"

"Archie- *Naah*. Reminds me of Harry and Meghan!" grinned Bhavna.

"Hmm. Anamika. Perfect for you- you cannot be named," grinned Reena as she ducked another flying pillow that came her way. "What about Aradhna? Arohi? Aakriti? Amita? Amrita?"

"Nooooo too old fashioned," smirked Bhavna. "I might as well stick to Bhavna then. Are you even looking at modern names? These are so 70`s and 80`s"

"*Di yaar*, Of course I am. Ok, what about Ahaana? Or Aisha? Anya? Aalia? Aalia is good, it`s simple short, and sweet."

"No *rey* Aalia is too filmy. Everyone will think of the actress Aalia Bhatt. Hmm, let me think about Ahaana. You think I look and sound like Ahaana?" she critically analysed herself in the mirror.

Reena by now was fast losing her cool, "what do you mean look and sound like Ahaana? What does it even mean?"

"I mean the name should suit me *na*. Ahaana..

Hmmm lyrical. But, what can Vikas call me endearingly? Aha? or Aana?" Eeeks, nooo this doesn`t work at all. Ahaana-cancel. This is so annoying. I mean how difficult can it be to choose your own name?" Bhavna kicked the edge of the bed.

Reena closed the laptop with a thud and kept it aside. She crossed her legs, and looked Bhavna in the eye, "*Di*!! let me give you a simple solution. You be who you are- Bhavna. OK. Ask *Panditji* to suggest an alphabet that would be a perfect match for Bhavna and then let Vikki *Jiju* change his name for you! After all his identity will change too *na*? He will be a husband and a son-in-law. Stars can be perfectly aligned from his end too, can`t they?"

Bhavna looked at her younger sister and pondered. Sometimes Reena did make sense. Why had she agreed to change her name? She may have had reservations about the name Bhavna but she had now accepted herself as Bhavna and was happy being herself. Bhavna picked up her phone and dialled Vikas.

there is enough treachery, hatred violence

absurdity in the average human being

 to supply any given army on any given day

Charles Bukowski

Laajo

It was scorching hot outside and though it was 10 in the morning, the humidity was unbearable and beads of perspiration shone on Laajo's forehead. She was running about to get all the chores done in time. Shyam and his family were to come at 11 a.m.

"These boys side people," muttered Laajo- They will only do what they like. Why couldn't they come in the evening? It's a little pleasant in the evening and even Neela's dad would not have to take a leave. He threw such a fuss, "Why do I have to be here for viewing? You women can manage it." She had to pull up her emotional card to pacify him, 'Of course, we can, but you know *Didi's* situation. She's a widow. There's no one to stand by her from her in-law's side. If the boy`s side sees you they will know there is someone to support in the future. If not for me and *Didi*, at least think of the poor girl. It's just for a couple of hours. You leave after lunch." He grunted and Laajo knew that the matter had settled in her favour.

Didi had always stood by her and did whatever she could to ease life for Laajo. Whether, it was during the birth of her children, the funeral of her in-laws, or her younger sister-in-law's wedding preparations. *Didi* always stepped in to manage the kitchen and household chores efficiently. This was her chance to pay back *Didi* for all she had done over the years. Surely, she could ensure that Chando got married to a decent boy.

Laajo was almost done with the preparations. She ran to the room that opened in the veranda and switched on the cooler-not that the old contraption helped much- even the *Kabadiwala* (scrap dealer) would not touch it- useless just like that Ramu who had been serving in their house for nearly a decade. That lazy lump Ramu wouldn't lift a finger if she weren't around. Such a tiresome fellow. But then at least she could dump the menial chores on him. Even the most useless people have some utility value. "Neela! O Neela. Are you all ready or not? It's almost eleven, my dear Miss India."

"Ma! Don't worry. Just a few minutes. Come see

how pretty our Chando looks" The excitement in Neela`s voice was palpable. Laajo walked into the room and critically evaluated Chando. Now what to say about this Chando? God is merciless- first, he gives the poor girl a lower-middle-class family, and then to top the misery- no physical beauty. *Na ji* nothing. An average girl. Neither too tall nor too short, neither fat nor thin, neither fair nor dark, neither sharp features nor dull ones. Just average. Graduate. B.A. in Hindi. Teacher in a private school. Ordinary girl. It was really tough to find a match for a girl like this. She was nearly nine months older than her Neela but looked much older than her 28 years.

Her eyes wavered towards Neela. Now that is what you call a girl! Tall, slim, and fair. Just last month Neela got engaged to Ashish who was currently posted in a big bank in *Bambai*- Mumbai whatever. His *bua ji* told Neela's dad the next posting would be overseas. Maybe Singapore or even Hong Kong! Laajo`s eyes sparkled with joy- Oh my Neela. What a blessing she is! And so lucky, imagine an educated handsome, and fairly rich boy -who would get a posting overseas- had picked her Neela.

"Ma," Neela`s sharp call broke her reverie, "Look at Chando, not me. She`s looking so good. Should I darken the lipstick a little more?"

"No need. She's looking nice," Laajo said curtly, "We can't doll her up much. Let them see what she really looks like. We don't want any problems later.

Let me go and see *Didi*. Why is she taking so long? *Didi*, O *Didi*," she called out as she stepped out of the room.

"Laajo, I am here in the kitchen."

"*Didi,* what are you doing? Stop helping this *nikkama* Ramu. Come on, spruce yourself a bit. The boy`s side will be here any minute." Laajo pulled at her hand.

"But what's wrong with what I am wearing? It`s simple and presentable," Didi looked at her neatly pinned saree.

Laajo snorted, "At least today, wear something nicer than this beige cotton saree you wear all the time, and tie your hair neatly in a bun."

"Laajo, they are coming to see my daughter- not me!" *Didi* smiled.

"I know," said Laajo condescendingly- "but even the mother has to look nice. Haven`t you heard the saying that if you want to marry a girl, look at her mother?"

Laajo watched her *Didi* lovingly. Poor *Didi*. Such a tough life she had had. Widowed at just 27 years. Chando was barely two years old when *Jijaji*`s scooter rammed into the truck on a highway. All *Didi* was left with was an infant, a small two-room apartment, old in-laws, and a measly pension from the government- *Jijaji* was a lowly paid Engineer in PWD. *Didi* took up a part-time job at a local sewing school, and between serving her in-laws and bringing up her daughter, she spent her life. A few years back she lost her in-laws and now it was just the two of them. Chando now worked in a local nursery school, so they managed a simple life with her earnings and *Jijaji*`s pension. Laajo was fortunately blessed with a large-hearted rich husband and she tried to help *Didi* financially as much as she could.

After Neela's engagement, Didi had become very restless. Her Chando was twenty-eight but there were hardly any *rishtas* for her. Who would want a simpleton from a poor family? Laajo knew she had to bail out *Didi* again and she instructed Neela's dad that he`d have to find someone for Chando now. Neela`s dad had approached a local *pandit* who had suggested that they should consider Shyam as a prospective groom for Chando.   Shyam was an engineer in a private firm and drew a decent salary. His family lived in Saharanpur but he had recently been transferred to Kanpur. Good. Chando won't have in-laws breathing down her neck. Laajo gave the go-ahead and the viewing had been scheduled for today.

***

It was five past eleven when the bell rang. Laajo smiled- so punctual. She greeted, "*Namaste*. Please come in." After exchanging pleasantries, Laajo motioned Chando to offer tea and snacks to all. The meeting progressed well. Shyam's mother had a relaxed look- she was smiling- and his father sipped his tea contentedly. Lajjo sighed with relief. Things were looking positive. "Aunty *ji* can I talk to Chando for five minutes?" Shyam asked Laajo respectfully. "Yes, of course, *beta. Kyu Didi*?" Laajo raised an eyebrow. Didi nodded her head affirmatively. Shyam walked into the room and Chando followed. She sat down on the chair looking down as she had been instructed. "Chando- you are not marrying me out of any compulsion, are you?" Shyam spoke gently.

Chando mumbled, "Nothing like that."

Shyam sighed with relief- "Good! I just wanted to clarify- Rahul is very young and I am sure he will adapt and take to you but I wanted to be sure that you are willing to take this forward." Chando was puzzled, "What do you mean? Who is Rahul?"

"My son."

Chando whispered, "You have a son? You are married?"

Shyam was startled, "I was. They haven't told you the details?

Chando nodded her head vigorously.

Shyam sighed, "I got divorced two years back. Poornima, my ex-wife, gave up Rahul's custody. He is almost four years old and stays with my parents. After our wedding, I will take him to Kanpur with us. There are better schools and facilities for children."

Chando`s mind whirred as she struggled to make sense of the situation. How could they do this to her? A divorcee with a child. I mean why would Mausi even consider this proposal? And why would they keep this information from me?

Shyam looked at her pained expression and knew there was no point in continuing. He got up and walked out.

"Let's go," he told his parents and they immediately scrambled on their feet.

"Arrey *beta* what happened? *Behenji* one minute- please sit. Whatever it is we will solve it." Laajo tried to stop them but they walked out briskly.

Didi, Laajo, and Neela, all rushed into the room. "Chando," Laajo screamed. "What did you say? Why did he walk away? They had almost agreed. How could you do this to us?"

"How could you do this to me, *Mausi*? What did you want me to do? Say yes to a divorcee who has a 4-year-old son? Why *Mausi*? And Maa you also…" Chando`s voice dripped with anguish.

Didi froze. She turned toward Laajo with a questioning look. Laajo looked away and said caustically "So what do you want?" Have you seen your position? Have you ever looked; I mean really looked at yourself in the mirror? Wake up- you are no Cinderella, and no Prince Charming is pining for you. You are already 28. Almost 29. You know how tough it is to find a suitable boy for a girl that old?"

"*Mausi*," Chando's voice trembled as she whispered, "Would you recommend a divorcee for Neela?

"Enough! Stop right there Chando," Laajo said coldly. "How dare you compare yourself to Neela? She has a rich father, and she is pretty- so not a word about Neela. People should know where they stand in life. I have always supported you but that doesn't mean you are on par with Neela. Shyam agreed to marry you- you should have been grateful to him! Today I realize the wisdom of what Amma ji would say, "Don't help these so-called poor helpless people. They are like the notorious camel- you give them an inch and they want the whole yard..."

Neela screamed, "Maa, please. What are you saying? Calm down."

Didi felt someone had punched her hard and sucked the life out of her. That someone was her younger richer sister- Laajo. She looked at Laajo and searched for her sister. But she couldn't find her.

She walked with leaden steps towards Chando and embraced her. Chando let out a sob, *Didi* patted her and they both clung to each other. Laajo stood rooted. She knew she had let arrogance and pride come in the way of love. There was no going back. *Didi* held Chando's hand firmly and they walked out of the house.

You may shoot me with your words,
You may cut me with your eyes,
You may kill me with your hatefulness,
But still, like air, I'll rise.

Maya Angelou

Tara

C handa, do you want some tea?' hollered Mrs Verma.

'*Ji bibiji*,' Chanda's muffled reply came from the courtyard. She was sweeping the veranda with firm energetic strokes, her thin frame swaying with each stroke. She had made a tidy heap of dried leaves, twigs, and little pebbles- all remnants of the storm that blew almost everything away last night. She placed her broom in one corner of the courtyard and walked up to the steps leading to the corridor outside the main house. Mehri came with some water in a steel jug.

*"Oi m*ove. Don`t stand so close", Mehri said sternly

while Chanda adjusted her faded cotton *dupatta* tied across her waist and smiled. "I am standing far. Stop complaining. Come on, pour some water now." Mehri stepped back, extended her hand, clutching tightly onto the jug handle, and hurriedly poured the water. Chanda washed her dirty hands vigorously. A thin stream of water trickled down her hands right up to her armpits. She then cupped her palms and gulped the cool water. "Can I have some more?" she asked as Mehri walked back towards the kitchen with the empty jug. Mehri snorted.

Just then Mrs. Verma strolled out of the house into the courtyard and called out, "Anu, *oi* Anu, where is my chair? Chanda, why are you standing near the steps? Did that Mehri give you tea or not?'
"No *bibiji*- not yet. She gave me water; I have asked her for some more."
"*Oh ho*, how much water do you drink? It seems like you lived in a desert during your last birth. Forever thirsty," Mrs Verma cackled. Chanda wanted to tell her that water kept hunger at bay, but refrained. Hunger and deprivation were her constant companions; she had learned to live with them. No point in telling these rich and high-caste people about it, they had never faced it.

Anu got a big cane chair with wooden armrests and placed it in the courtyard near the steps. Mrs Verma sank into it and sighed, "…and this Mehri also I tell you- absolutely useless. I don't know why only I have to get all these lazy servants. Sit there, Chanda, so I can see you when I talk to you," she pointed to one corner of the courtyard. "Tell me about your daughter. How old is she now? Sixteen? Why don't you bring her along with you? She should be helping you. You are also getting old. How long can you go on like this, sweeping courtyards and cleaning bathrooms every day?"

Mrs. Verma loved chatting with all the house helpers. Once her husband left for work, she didn't have much to do except laze about, read magazines or watch TV, and of course talk to anyone and everyone around.

Chanda sat on her haunches a little away from Mrs. Verma. "You are right. I should get her along to help. But what to do *bibiji?* She is young and she is pretty. Actually, too pretty for her good. You know how lecherous these men can be. The *paanwala* at the corner of the lane is a real rascal. The way he eyed her the other day when she tagged along with me…" Chanda shivered. "We are poor sweepers *bibiji.* If anything happens then people blame us only. Even that old Parkash- who works for Jamshed *babu* is a creep."

Mrs. Verma perked, "Jamshed? that Siloo's son? How is he? I haven't seen him for years. I think he is a nice guy- but too simple. His brothers are the wicked ones. Jeroo and that other skinny one, what`s his name? Manik?" Mrs. Verma went on as Chanda nodded, "They have too much property I tell you. You know Chanda, half of this city once belonged to Jamshed`s grandfather. But his son did not keep it together; now they barely have a fraction of the wealth left. Quite useless I tell you. And these 3 grandsons are also of no good. Jeroo and Manik are devious I tell you. I have heard that they are trying to oust poor Jamshed. He only has two houses left in his share now. What the world has come to? Poor simple fellows are taken for a ride by their own family!" Mrs Verma went on with her rant.

Chanda didn't follow much but still nodded in agreement. Mrs. Verma was the only one who talked to her nicely, everyone else would frown and treat her high-handedly, for she was from the sweeper community- they called her *jamaadar.* Most people didn't let her near them, forget talking or offering tea. "Hmm Jamshed *babu* is really nice. He gives me tea every day. Sometimes bread also. You know *bibiji* he keeps the bread in his Godrej cupboard!" Chanda giggled. "Even biscuits and nuts. He keeps them in tin boxes. All of them locked up in his cupboard!" Mrs. Verma smirked 'Parsis are like that only, a little strange, Mr. Verma says everyone from the Parsi community is a little strange…and what did you say? He`s nice? just because he gives tea every day you say he is nice. What do you know about him? I tell you Chanda you are very simple; anyone can take you for a ride. One tea and you are floored. The world is very cruel- manipulative- I bet he makes you broom his courtyard every day- storm *or* no storm. And here I give you tea every day- and didn't I give you a few *pooris* just yesterday? But you never say Verma *bibiji* is very good- never-ever you say that. One cup of tea from that Jamshed and you sing his praises."

"*Na, Na bibiji*,' Chanda countered hastily. 'You ask the *paanwala*- or Sen *bibiji* or even Chadha *bibiji*- I always tell them how kind you are. You let me sit near you- you give me tea; see I got these red bangles with the money you gave me last week" Chanda waved her arms energetically. "You are very kind. I pray for your long life always."

Mrs. Verma smiled, "What to do? I am a soft-hearted person. We are all children of God. I really believe that the world is my family. Now tell me about your Chandini. What were you saying about her earlier?"

Chanda smiled, "*Bibiji* her name is Tara."

"Tara, Chandini, all the same only. So, what does she do the whole day then."

"Tara is a good daughter - does all the household chores. Never complains. No hanky-panky with boys. She can read, and write also some words in Hindi. She is so slim, pretty- long lovely hair-you know her plait is so thick! And she sings also. Everyone in my community says she sings like a nightingale. *Bibiji* they everyone says she is a heroine," gushed Chanda. Mrs. Verma smiled, "You are such a simpleton. All of us find our children very beautiful." Chanda continued, "I'm now looking out for a boy for her. She is almost eighteen. I asked Mehri and even Anu if they could suggest a good boy for Tara. They both turned up their noses and said they didn't know of any suitable boys. *Bibiji* do you know of anyone for my Tara?"

Mrs. Verma smirked, "And where can I find a boy for her? As for Anu and all, you know they all belong to a higher caste than yours." Chanda's face fell, "*Haan bibiji*. That is true. Anu and Mehri don't even let me sit near them. Not everyone is like you *Bibiji*. Overlooking caste difference. Can you not ask *Sahab* if he has anyone in the office- any nice boy?"

"Alright Chanda,' Mrs. Verma said brusquely. She knew it was time to close the conversation else this Chanda would pester her to find a suitable boy for her daughter. "Clean the shed outside properly. There is too much dust because of the storm last night. Anu, give Chanda some tea. Give her a biscuit also from that tin box kept outside the kitchen".

Mrs. Verma clutched onto the armrest, heaved herself up, and waddled back to the main house. Anu came with some tea in a steel glass. Chanda got up and picked a chipped brown cup with no handle and kept it on the steps. She stepped away while Anu poured the tea from the glass, and a few drops splattered on the ground. She placed a few broken pieces of biscuit on a torn piece of newspaper and kept it near Chanda. Chanda sighed as she absently ate the soggy biscuit and gulped the lukewarm tea. She knew Mrs Verma could not help her, but as a mother, she had to knock all possible doors to get a nice groom for her Tara. At least Mrs. Verma treated her kindly.

She sighed. She had long accepted her fate. She was destined to live this life of drudgery and shame. No one could help her. But she still dreamt of a better future for Tara. Though most days, she was sure that Tara would eventually marry someone from her community, and this cycle would continue. God had given up on her. He had made her a sweeper. Then why blame other people- He only had made them other people! She finished the tea, rinsed her cup, kept it near the shed, picked up her broom, and walked out. She still had to clean three more houses.

***

Mrs. Verma called out, "Tara, O Tara, you want some tea?"

"Ji bibiji." chimed Tara, and she quickly finished sweeping the courtyard. She rested her broom neatly in one corner of the courtyard and walked towards the steps leading to the main house. She stood

dutifully as Mehri poured water from the steel jug onto her hands, and she vigorously washed them. She cupped her palms, took big gulps of the cool water, and then splashed a little water on her face. She untied her faded cotton dupatta from her waist, wiped her face, walked to the other end of the courtyard, and sat on her haunches. She placed the chipped brown mug a little away from herself as Anu came with some tea in a steel glass and poured it into the mug; a few drops splashed on the floor.

Tara waited respectfully till Anu walked back. She then grabbed the mug and wrapped her palms around the cup. Ah! The aroma of tea filled her with pleasure. She slurped hungrily as the hot sweet tea slid down her throat. She liked Anu. She always gave her hot tea. Tara savored each sip. Mrs. Verma walked towards her and placed a torn piece of newspaper next to her. A few broken pieces of different kinds of biscuits lay strewn on it.

"Here. Eat."

Tara looked at her with gratitude. Her stomach rumbled in anticipation of food. The soggy, moist biscuits turned soft and mushy as she gingerly dunked them in hot tea.

"How is your mother?" inquired Mrs. Verma as she sank into the armchair.

Tara popped a piece of biscuit in her mouth and replied, "She is still weak. The doctor at the municipality said she would take some time to recover. She has malaria. Too many mosquitos in our area."

Mrs. Verma snorted, "why do all live in such filth? Can you not sweep and clean your own houses?"

"Ji *Bibiji.* We try but…it's a slum. How much can we clean it?" Tara shrugged.

"Hmm," grunted Mrs. Verma. She looked at Tara as she slurped on the sweet tea, wisps of hair blowing across her round face, and the thought struck her- Tara was pretty. Very pretty. She rebuked her, "And you be careful. Cover your chest well. Open the *dupatta* and wear it properly when you go to other houses- especially Jamshed's house. That Prakash who works for him is a creep. You have to take care of yourself. These men are absolute rouges."

Tara felt a warm blush rising on her neck and rapidly proceeding to her cheeks. She looked down and nodded. She finished her tea, rinsed the cup, placed it near the shed, and almost ran out. There were too many jobs to be done; besides, she didn't want to talk about working at Jamshed`s house. Mrs. Verma was nosy and would keep digging for information for no reason.

***

"Where has this girl Tara disappeared? She's not

turned up today also. Four days in a row- who does that?" Mrs Verma snapped irately at Anu.

"*Bibiji,* who to ask?" Anu shrugged helplessly.

"Go to that Jamshed`s house. Ask that Prakash. Has she been going there and not turning up here? I tell you, these people are capable of just anything!" Mrs. Verma lashed as Anu stood wringing her hands in despair.

"*Bibiji,* I had gone there last evening. His house was locked."

"Then ask that *paanwala* at the corner. Chanda buys tobacco from him. He knows her and Tara."

"I asked him too last evening, and he said he hasn't seen her either. And *bibiji,* you know that we don't talk to these sweepers, so how would I know about her whereabouts?"

"Hmmm" frowned Mrs. Verma as she sprawled on the cane chair sipping sweet tea. She heard the tinkling of bangles. "Is someone outside?"

"*Ji bibiji,*" called out Chanda.

"Chanda? You are back. Wait there, I am coming." Mrs. Verma dawdled into the courtyard and sprawled on the cane chair. Chanda stood in a corner, respectfully. "Where is that useless daughter of yours? And you have recovered?" she remarked caustically as she saw Chanda dressed in a clean bright pink *salwar kurta* with a *dupatta* covering her head.

Chanda`s red bangles twinkled as she walked

towards Mrs Verma with a small bright cardboard box in her hand. She kept it next to Mrs. Verma`s feet and smiled widely, "*Bibiji,* I got sweets for you. Tara got married. Sorry, I could not invite anyone as it was a very rushed affair. You see Tara eloped and got married in the court. I was very happy about it, but our community would not accept this wedding. It took me 3 full days to convince the elders of our community. He doesn`t belong to our caste *na.* Yesterday we got them married according to our rituals and then I hosted a feast for all of them. Do eat the sweets, *Bibiji,* and bless her. God is very kind." Chanda`s eyes were brimming with tears.

Mrs. Verma looked disdainfully at the cheap red cardboard box full of sweets. "Anu," she called out, "take this box." Anu came and reluctantly picked up the box and kept it on the stool outside the kitchen. Mrs. Verma removed a small pouch from her blouse, pulled out a hundred-rupee note, and kept it on the floor. "Here. Take this. Give it to Tara."

Chanda folded her palms and bowed respectfully, "May God give you a long life *Bibiji,*" and quickly grabbed the note before it could fly away with the wind. "Tara is waiting outside only. She wants your blessings, but she is feeling very shy, so she is standing outside," Chanda said breathlessly.

"Call her, let me see how she looks as a new bride," Mrs Verma smiled.

"Tara, come in dear," Chanda called out loudly.

"Tell Mehri to get some tea for Chanda and Tara," Mrs. Verma instructed Anu.

Anu scowled and went inside the kitchen. Tara walked inside the *aangan,* wearing a brightly embroidered red *salwar kurta* with a shimmering *dupatta* draped across her chest. Crimson red vermilion streaked across the parting of her hair, a big round *bindi* on her forehead, shiny red lips, golden hoops in her ears that twinkled as the sun rays fell on her smiling face.

"Namaste bibiji," she smiled coyly.

"You make a pretty bride, Tara. How is your new husband? Love marriage *haan*? And I thought you were a simple girl." Mrs. Verma winked and smiled. "Sit. Anu is getting some tea. Where is the boy from? What is his name?"

Tara blushed as she walked towards Mrs Verma. She pulled a chair from the other corner and sat next to her. *"Jamshed,"* she replied coyly.

Mrs Verma sat stunned as Tara pulled another chair and motioned Chanda to sit next to her.

.

ABOUT THE AUTHOR

Aarti Punjabi is a Mumbai-based storyteller, writer, and podcaster, who loves to perform stories and Spoken word pieces in Hindi and English. She narrates Hindi stories on her podcast *Kahani Humari Tumhari* across various audio platforms. She loves to sing and enjoy a cuppa with friends when she's not reading or writing.

You may write to her at aartimpunjabi@gmail.com or follow her Instagram handle arty.punjabi

Printed in Dunstable, United Kingdom